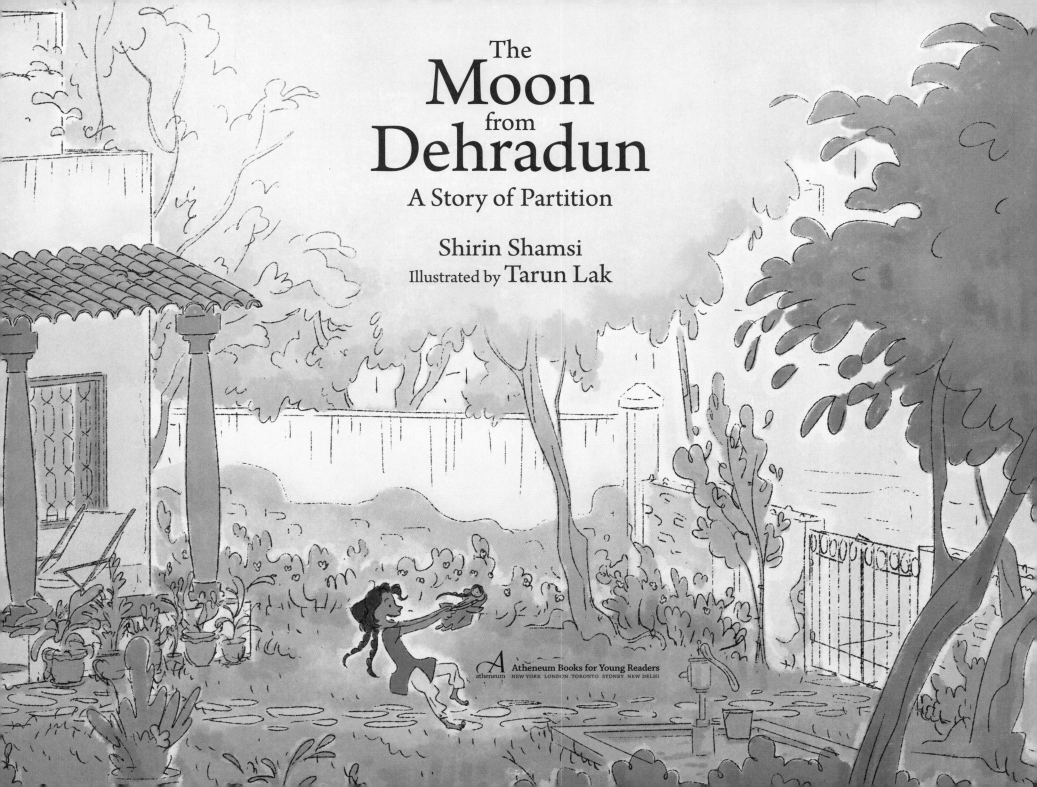

The Moon
from
Dehradun

A Story of Partition

Shirin Shamsi

Illustrated by Tarun Lak

Atheneum Books for Young Readers
NEW YORK LONDON TORONTO SYDNEY NEW DELHI

Dehradun has always been home. My daada was born here, and his daada before him. And Gurya has been with me since I was born—since Daadi made her from the softest cotton, with bright button eyes and a long woolen braid.

I wrap her soft and snug in Ammi's shawl.

"We are moving," I whisper in her ear. "In five days, we will go on a train ride."

I arrange sweet-scented flowers in her hair.

There is shouting outside.
"Why are people angry?" I ask.
"They are afraid," Ammi says, "because
our home has been divided, and some of them
don't know where they belong anymore."

When Ammi makes halva, she cuts
it into pieces.
Can that happen to a place?

Noises from the street awaken
my baby brother. He cries.
"Azra," Ammi calls. "Bring Chotu."
I put Gurya on the bed and lift
Chotu into my arms. His drool stains
my kurta. I wrinkle my nose.

Ammi stirs the simmering pot. My tummy growls, but we must wait for Abba to return with our tickets.

The noise outside grows louder. Chotu reaches for Ammi. Abba arrives. Breathless, he wipes sweat off his forehead.

"We must leave now," Abba says. "There is a train leaving for Lahore tonight."

"But what about dinner?" I ask.

"There's no time to eat. It's not safe. We cannot wait another day."

Ammi turns off the fire. Daal chawal sits in a pot, warm on the stove. Fluffy buttered rice, ready to eat. My empty tummy fills with fear.

Ammi looks around. No time to pack.
She sighs and slips her rehl into a cloth bag.
Chotu wriggles as I hold him. Gently,
Ammi takes him from me.

Through the verandah to the back gate, we make
our way to where Abba waits. He lifts us into the truck.
Hot, sticky, huddled together.
　　Across the street, a new flag flutters in the wind.

"Gurya," I yell. "We left Gurya!"
"We cannot go back," Abba whispers.

The muezzin's call echoes from the minaret. I think it sounds like a sad goodbye. The fruit seller's cart sits empty on the street. The dhobi sits quietly. Bibi-jee holds a tasbih in her hand, her lips moving in prayer.

I stare at Chotu fiercely. It's all his fault.
He made me forget.

The truck races fast down the road. My heart races too, and the moon chases after us.

I turn to Ammi for a hug, but her arms are wrapped tight around Chotu.

I would wrap my arms around Gurya and hold her close to my heart. But my arms are empty, and my eyes fill with tears.

At the station, we board the train. Wheels screech along the tracks as we pull away. Away from home. Away from Gurya.
My heart sinks like a stone in a well.

Clickety-clack, chugging along the track.
We cannot go back.

I look around, and a sea of faces stares back at me.
"Why is everyone sad?" I ask Ammi.
"When something breaks, it takes time to heal," Ammi whispers.

A piece of me also feels broken.

Days and nights pass. Chotu cries, restless to be free. He wriggles from Ammi's lap as she sleeps. I follow him as he crawls.

I pull him into my arms.
"Look Chotu." I point out the window.
"Look—chand. It has followed us from Dehradun."
It will be shining down on Gurya. I wish she
were here. She will be afraid without me.

Chotu hides his face in my shoulder.

"Are you afraid too?" I ask. He sniffles and looks at me. I see my face mirrored in his eyes. Maybe he misses home too. Maybe he needs me also.

"It's okay," I tell him gently, even though he drools on me again.

Hissing, the train shudders to a stop. Strangers offer us water and chapatis that taste better than the best feast on Eid.

I give Chotu a sip first, then I take a long gulp.

We stand in line until my legs are sore. My kurta sticks to my skin with dust and sweat. An officer checks our papers and gives Abba new ones for a home here in Lahore.

Silence greets us like a shadow in our new
house. Empty rooms. Clothes scattered.
Did this family also leave in a hurry?

In the kitchen, a pot of daal sits on the stove.
Cold and stale.
Ammi and Abba are quiet.
Chotu crawls happily on the hard tiles, and
I follow him deeper into the house.

When he stops at a door and turns to me, I kneel on the ground beside him, wrapping him in a hug warmer than Gurya's had ever been. "We'll be okay."

I pick him up and push the door open. It leads to a verandah. I breathe in the sweet-scented flowers growing on a vine. I close my eyes and remember.
  "Chotu, we are home," I say.

A knock at the door startles us all.
"Who is that?" Ammi calls.
Abba answers the door.
"Assalaamu-alaikum."

Our new neighbors enter with
hot food and warm smiles.
Sweet halva-poori and spicy cholay.

We sit together, gathered on a dhurrie.
Sharing food, strangers become friends.

In the bedroom at night, I find a sad-looking doll, worn and ragged.
"Were you forgotten too?" I whisper, wrapping the doll in my shawl and holding her close to my heart. "Don't worry, I'll keep you safe." Maybe someone will take care of my Gurya, too.

The stars shine down with light enough for everyone.

A muezzin's call to prayer echoes through an open window like a hopeful hello.

And the moon is still at last.

THE PARTITION OF INDIA, 1947

This map is a depiction of the 1947 division of the Indian subcontinent as demarcated by the Radcliffe Line. Named after its architect, Lord Cyril Radcliffe, it separated the modern nations of India and Pakistan, though the borders were crudely drawn, and would lead to further conflict and violence decades after its creation. Larger princely states like Hyderabad and Kalat would eventually join the nations that surrounded them, while East Pakistan would win a war of independence against Pakistan to become Bangladesh in 1972. Kashmir remains in dispute.

Kashmir

Lahore

WEST PAKISTAN

Punjab

Dehradun

Kalat

RADCLIFFE LINE

Sikkim

RADCLIFFE LINE

EAST PAKISTAN

Gwadar

INDIA

Junagadh

Dadra and Nagar Haveli

Daman and Diu

BAY OF BENGAL

Hyderabad

Goa

Puducherry

INDIAN OCEAN

Inset map

Kashmir

WEST PAKISTAN

Lahore

AZRA'S JOURNEY

Punjab

Dehradun

RADCLIFFE LINE

INDIA

GLOSSARY

abba: father

ammi: mother

assalaamu-alaikum: Muslim greeting meaning "peace be with you"

bibi-jee: term of respect for an elderly woman

chand: moon

chapatis: round flatbread

chawal: rice

cholay: chickpeas

chotu: term of endearment meaning "little one"

daal: lentils

daada: paternal grandfather

daadi: paternal grandmother

Dehradun: city in Uttarakhand, India

dhobi: traditionally, a person who provides a laundry service

dhurrie: rug

Eid: festival

gurya: doll

halva-poori: sweet dessert often made from semolina, with fried flatbread

kurta: shirt/dress

Lahore: city in Punjab, Pakistan

muezzin: one who makes a call to prayer from the mosque—through a loudspeaker, the call can be heard far and wide

rehl: wooden book stand used for reading the Holy Quran

tasbih: beads threaded on a string, used in prayer

PRE-PARTITION

The Indian subcontinent was once a place of many kingdoms rich in spices, fabrics, and jewels. The British first arrived during the 1600s with the East India Company to colonize the land, stealing its resources and wealth for themselves, growing rich and powerful by exploiting locals. By the 1850s, people were fed up with the mistreatment. Peasants, workers, and soldiers alike took up arms against their invaders. But the Rebellion of 1857, as this came to be known, was brutally stamped out by the colonial administration.

Seeing how powerful a united group could be, the British implemented policies to divide the subcontinent's diverse, peacefully coexisting population to prevent them from allying again and threatening colonial rule. These policies of "divide and conquer" are believed by many to be the underlying cause of Partition.

PARTITION

In 1947, British India finally achieved independence. But the British never unified the subcontinent— which had always been a patchwork of hundreds of princely states—and the problems that were seeded by their policy of division remained. So after centuries of colonial rule, British India was partitioned into separate nations.

The British partitioned hastily, leaving only two months for the newly independent governments of India and Pakistan to figure out the details. Then they withdrew entirely, not even publicizing the borders until after the partition was announced. Many people did not know in which country their homes belonged. While the government was being divided, armed gangs, which had embraced ideals of violence and fascism during World War II, roamed freely, destroying lives and communities. Fear and anxiety were rampant, and millions of families decided to flee. Many hoped it would only be temporary, even leaving their valuables behind.

Few knew then what the consequences would be, or that for many, it was their last time seeing their homelands. The haste of British withdrawal, and the uncertainty it left behind, created chaos and lawlessness. Leaders had no control over vigilante

militias. The brutality and bloodshed endured by refugees who crossed the newly drawn borders have led to a mistrust that still exists today. As a result, the border between India and Pakistan is one of the most militarized in the world, heavily armed with nuclear warheads, and visible even from space.

MY FAMILY'S STORY

This story was inspired by my mother's childhood experience, when violence came to her family's beautiful town nestled in the foothills of the Himalayas. Her parents made the decision to leave their home and travel to the newly independent republic of Pakistan. My mother, Perveen, traveled with her parents and siblings—Mamu Aziz, Khala Nasreen, Khala Azra, and Mamu Saeed—by train from Dehradun to Lahore.

In the account my mother relayed to me, her journey was filled with uncertainty, terror, and fear. She remembers the train passing desolate villages with bodies on the ground and people traveling on foot or on bullock carts, fleeing to safety. At one point, their train was attacked, and everyone hid beneath the seats. There was an army platoon on their train, so they were protected, and theirs was the first train to arrive safely—the first to have survivors. The atmosphere was celebratory as their train pulled into a small station across the border, just before Lahore. People cheered and jumped onto the train to welcome them with food, lassi, and water, relieved and happy to see them safe and well.

This story honors my parents, their families, and all the lives that were lost or displaced during the Partition of 1947. I wish to honor their resilience and commitment to rebuilding promising futures for their children in their new homelands. I hope that by recognizing these personal tragedies on each side of the border, we can build bridges of understanding, tolerance, respect, and a commitment to a peaceful and harmonious future. With unity and friendship, so much can be achieved. 　　　　　　—s. s.

پیاری امی جان کے نام

To my mother, whose childhood experience
of Partition inspired this story
—S. S.

To my family, and all those who
were displaced during the partition
—T. L.

𝒜
atheneum

ATHENEUM BOOKS FOR YOUNG READERS

An imprint of Simon & Schuster Children's Publishing Division • 1230 Avenue of the Americas, New York, New York 10020 • Text © 2022 by Shirin Shamsi • Illustration © 2022 by Tarun Lak • Book design © 2022 by Simon & Schuster, Inc. • All rights reserved, including the right of reproduction in whole or in part in any form. • ATHENEUM BOOKS FOR YOUNG READERS is a registered trademark of Simon & Schuster, Inc. • Atheneum logo is a trademark of Simon & Schuster, Inc. • For information about special discounts for bulk purchases, please contact Simon & Schuster Special Sales at 1-866-506-1949 or business@simonandschuster.com. • The Simon & Schuster Speakers Bureau can bring authors to your live event. For more information or to book an event, contact the Simon & Schuster Speakers Bureau at 1-866-248-3049 or visit our website at www.simonspeakers.com. • The text for this book was set in Arno Pro. • The illustrations for this book were rendered digitally. • Manufactured in Hong Kong • 0422 SCP • First Edition • 10 9 8 7 6 5 4 3 2 1 • Library of Congress Cataloging-in-Publication Data • Names: Shamsi, Shirin, author. | Lak, Tarun, illustrator. • Title: The moon from Dehradun : a story of partition / Shirin Shamsi ; illustrated by Tarun Lak. • Description: First edition. | New York : Atheneum Books for Young Readers, [2022] | Audience: Ages 4–8. | Audience: Grades 2–3. | Summary: A young girl leaves her beloved doll behind when she must make the journey from India to Pakistan in the aftermath of their partition by the British government. • Identifiers: LCCN 2021048796 (print) | LCCN 2021048797 (ebook) | ISBN 9781665906791 (hardcover) | ISBN 9781665906807 (ebook) • Subjects: CYAC: Refugees—Fiction. | Muslims—Fiction. | India—History—Partition, 1947—Fiction. | LCGFT: Picture books. • Classification: LCC PZ7.1.S479 Mo 2022 (print) | LCC PZ7.1.S479 (ebook) | DDC [E]—dc23 • LC record available at https://lccn.loc.gov/2021048796 • LC ebook record available at https://lccn.loc.gov/2021048797